INTO THE WOODS OF ORIENT HILLS

Amidst the tranquillity of the hills is something very sinister

SAI CHANDER AKULA

INDIA • SINGAPORE • MALAYSIA

It's not just one day, I would consider this as one more day to cherish your goodness. You've been kind hearted to many with your good heart and positive deeds.

I would take this opportunity to dedicate the book to my beloved father who is not around us but his name and soul is always with us.

Thank you for everything you provided us, memories with you will be cherished for entire life.

With love from

– Sai Chander Akula

Chapter 1

Orient hills were the place for peace and security for many decades, residents of the hills enjoyed life with prosperity but one incident shook the entire town. There was a big storm on the way that residents of the town never imagined. There were 500 houses and 200 cottages in the town and it was a beautiful place for living. But all these attributes were in the past, currently two innocent residents were murdered brutally and orient hills were silent witness for these killings.

The blood shed occurred in a cottage located in southern part of the town, cottage named as "Ivy and Mike love". Ivy and Mike were two civilians who were killed without any mercy.

Cottage was an absolute beautiful one perfectly furnished, beautiful garden in front of the house and customized swimming pool for relaxing. They had a dog which was a German shepherd and it was good enough for their silent company.

This incident shook entire town shelters and crowd started to gather near cottage to see how murders happened. Meanwhile news spread faster and police of the orient hills were given a message about the incident. Vikram sen was made in-charge of the investigation and higher authorities needs his assistance badly. Vikram was suspended for 3 months for making an injury to an accused in the course of investigation but his expertise in handling murder investigations was irreplaceable. Presently, vikram is at the bar consuming alcohol so that he forgets his mental injuries. His mobile rings and he answered for the second one.

"Hello" he says.

"Vikram, this is pratap" pratap is superior to him.

"Yes sir!" says vikram.

"There is a murder of two couples in orient hills and we need your assistance" he adds.

"Sir, are you kidding?"

"I'm suspended and not interested in this job anymore"

"I'm helpless, please forgive me!" vikram adds.

"I know the pain you're going through but we are in hell due to these murders"

"Please report immediately and I'll make sure your suspension is revoked" pratap confirms.

"Sir, I'm at the bar and high in alcohol"

"Can't make out today"

"Okay, report to office in the first hour of morning" says pratap.

"Sure Sir!" he finally adds.

Vikram was overloaded and bar management drops him safely in his home. Pratap makes arrangements for the safeguard of bodies and clues at the cottage without been wiped out.

Chapter 2

Bar management drops vikram at his place as he was high in alcohol. Over consumption of alcohol made him late in his work, pratap made sure clues were safe without been destroyed.

Vikram had reached cottage to take in charge of the murder. Seeing the blood shed he couldn't resist and vomits nearby. Throats of bodies were cut brutally and were thrown into the pool. Blood from the bodies spread across the pool making red and it resembled the night of red moon. Ivy and Jake were killed in living room and dragged till pool until thrown away. Blood stains were on the walls and every place in the room. Vikram ordered his subordinates to extract the bodies from the pool.

"Extract the bodies carefully and I want them dam accurate"

"If needed help, let me know so that I'll put myself" says vikram.

Govind was the subordinate and managed to pull of the task.

Vikram calls for clues team to take ownership of the clues without been wiped out. When bodies were extracted it shocked entire police team including vikram as they were strange killings. Their eyes were peeled off and legs contained cuts of knives.

"So inhuman and no mercy, their eyes were peeled off and tortured brutally. Those bastards must be hanged to death" says govind.

"Yeah, so inhuman and brutal in nature" "I'll not leave them and show them their true destiny" says vikram.

As crowd started to increase more in numbers, he ordered everyone should be cleared so that there is no chaos. Clues team arrived and they started searching for clues with the help of vikram.

They were searching each and every corner of the house but it was in vain. Murderers were professional and they didn't leave any clue. This made job of vikram tougher but he was determined to find the culprits.

Even in a large desert, a small pond of water is more valuable and currently vikram experiencing the same but fortune brought him some luck. German shepherd was a clever dog and was deeply moved by the demise of owners. It can identify the murderers and immediately runs upstairs. In the balcony there were footprints which are suspicious and it's starts barking. Without wasting more time vikram observed footprints and these footprints were different in size and it was strange from an investigation point of view. Clues team ensures photographs are taken and samples are sent to forensic lab. Murderers used ladder to reach balcony and moved into living room.

"I can't understand how they entered and escaped??" says vikram.

Ladder was lying beside the garden area.

Then he slowly examined the garden area, while he was walking, he could hear an empty sound generated, when he stopped walking there wasn't any sound. He ordered his subordinates to search the area and when they dug, they found a secret passage to go out of the cottage. This was the passage which helped murderers to exit safely.

There were rumours everywhere in the town about the murder, vikram and his team ensured there is proper maintenance of law and order. Vikram reports to the office to explain his primary investigation.

"Sir, the murder seems to be very strange and it looks like someone has a strong reason to murder them. Looking at the bodies it depicts they were chased and killed brutally. There are also chances of murderer who is a psychopath. We will investigate and provide further details"

"Sure, let me know if you need any assistance" the superior confirmed.

"Sure sir"

"Thank you!" says vikram.

Vikram orders govind to extract the files of past murders which happened similar way. There were a large bunch of files and he asked his team to share the work and get back soon.

He drives back home with a bottle of alcohol to make his day relaxed. Suddenly his mobile rings and it was his mom. She resides 60 kms away from orient hills and a busy housewife. She's concerned about vikram and his rough attitude towards culprits and wants him to quit the job as it's not safe.

"Yes mom"

"Is everything fine??"

"I'm doing good, how about you?"

"I'm doing great"

"Are you having meals on time??" she questioned.

"Yes mom"

"Look at others, they're married and leading peaceful life with kids"

"Mom, please stop watching those serials. You're influenced with those and I'm passionate about doing my job" says vikram.

"I'm receiving an urgent call, please forgive me" and he disconnects.

He didn't receive any call though as his mom would kill him with the investigation. He enjoys alcohol and takes deep sleep after having his supper.

Chapter 3

Next day he reached office early to observe the progress of task. Team has reviewed only 20 files out of 89, he was angry and took everyone to dangerous ride with his words.

"Do you understand the severity of this case"

"If not please step forward I'll make you understand" says vikram.

"These murders caught the attention of higher officials and there is silent revolt uprising in public to find the murderer"

"Sorry sir" says one of the members.

"Sir, I've not reviewed the files but I can remember a case on lonely highway near woods"

"It's similar in nature"

"A lonely highway, what do you mean??" says vikram.

"Sir, there was a peculiar murder which happened on the highway near woods, since then the highway was lonely for few months and deserted during nights"

"A couple was killed brutally who were passing by and dragged into the woods. Their bodies were hanged to tree and offered few mysterious tantric poojas" he responded.

"Are you kidding, aren't you??"

"We are in the age of civilized culture and still do we have such superstitious traditions??" Vikram questioned.

"Yes sir, still we have few idiots who follow this" he adds.

"We shall go to that place and search if we could find any clue"

"Sure Sir" and vikram with his team reached the lonely highway.

Indeed, highway was resembling path to death, local residents near highway confirmed during nights they hear strange sounds and there would be strange screaming's. This made vikram to believe some suspicious activities were going in the town which were responsible for these killings.

Vikram and his team reach the woods and indeed they were very scary, ground was covered with thick layer of grass and it resembled mattress in a home. Trees were very high and close enough and perfect place of ill-legal activities, webs of spiders were so thick that it resembled as if layers of fog were formed. They start investigating each and every corner of murdered place to find out a clue which could help in investigation.

Then govind noticed few things which were mysterious, he found a doll which was pinned with needles and had strange markings on face of the doll, additionally decorative colours were thrown on the ground and doll was decorated in colour. Few distance from doll he also found a knife which had blood stains on it.

"Sir, please watch this, I've found a doll and a knife" says govind.

Without wasting time vikram becomes attentive and observes them. He orders subordinates to collect these and send them to forensic lab immediately. He also demands autopsy report of the murder which took place on lonely highway.

It was noon till they collected the evidences and send to the forensic lab. Weather was dry and it was hard for them to contact every resident near highway. Vikram assured them he could arrange night patrolling to stop these activities in the woods. He also assured them he could arrange street lights for night visibility. While this investigation continues, he ordered his subordinates to have lunch and meet him the office.

Vikram reached office to provide the status of investigation.

"Sir, this is clear case of some illegal activities which are going in the woods. We've found superstitious articles in the woods and murder of a couple in similar way to "jake and ivy" says vikram.

Hearing these words superior was shocked and was completely amazed with case progress.

"I'm granting full orders, take charge and close this case as soon as possible" says superior.

Vikram leaves his chamber and makes his way to home. It was a tired day and buys a pack of cigarettes for his routine smoking. When he reached home, he was completely shocked and was thrown into a well of uncertainty. He found few words written on the entrance door of house.

"Stay away otherwise you'll be at stake" these were the words written and they were red in colour. He carefully removes his gun and fires in the air. He could hear some footsteps running and immediately rushed towards the road, he found a person running and thought of firing but the target was in long distance. Suspicious person was grabbed in to the car by few persons and they escape. He reached entrance door, took his hand and placed on words, he smelled the blood and it was pertaining to an animal.

Chapter 4

Vikram was in the state of illusion "How can someone dare to give warning to police and in such unusual manner"

With this he understood someone is keeping an eye on his investigation and wanted to keep the details of investigation safer. Next day he ordered govind to keep the case details in a safe place with been accessible only to few. Meanwhile he receives a call from the residents near lonely highway claiming a disturbing sight. He immediately rushed to the place to take the charge and now it was a horrible view. The road was blocked with heads of goats and bodies were hanged with a rope horizontally. Blood was pouring from the bodies of goats and was clear indication of warning.

He bends down and touches the blood which was shattered on the road and he could sense some warm in it and concludes this was done just few hours ago.

"Search the place immediately within 5kms radius and bring to me if anyone found suspicious"

A team of 5 police personnel gets into action and moves on to find the them. Govind and vikram move into the woods to see if anything is found, but in vain. They move deeper into the woods but still no clue. When moved further they found few words "stay away" written on the trees and this was very disturbing for them. They return to highway and investigate one of the residents.

"What's your name??" vikram questions.

"Manohar" another person replies.

"Do you have anyone idea of this and who could be responsible??"

"I'm not sure sir but we have a gang which does notorious things in the town"

"A gang??" vikram with a face of surprise.

"Where do they stay??" He further added.

"They stay beside the railway tracks with temporary houses constructed with wooden, they won't stay in one place. They move in gang conducting illegal activities for their survival"

They claim themselves as "Griffins" and wore the jackets which has the picture of eagle.

"Please be careful in handling them, it's like entering the den of a lion without proper security" manohar adds.

"Don't worry, I'm the best in handling human lions" says vikram ironically.

Vikram and govind are now on the journey which is extremely dangerous and can take their life if not handled smoothly. They gather information about them through a secret agent and want to know about their daily life in the disguise of griffins. They finally reach the place dressed like griffins. When they enter the place, it was a different world for them. Place was untidy, some people were having cocaine which was secretly smuggled into town. They were 100 people and had the repository of smugglers, robbed products and other illegal substances. When they move further into the area passing by houses, they were found suspicious and stopped by a lady. Though she was a griffin her attractive eyes and seductive appearance made govind to fall for her. She wore a jeans and t shirt with a cigarette smoking.

"Who the hell are you?? I haven't seen you before" she questions.

Govind was speechless by her appearance and seeing this vikram adds.

"We are orphans and couldn't get the place in the town due to this, and our appearance also were untidy and this caused them to forcibly move us" vikram adds.

"Yes, I know the town residents are inhuman and they will repent soon for this" lady says.

"We thought this is the right place for us and we entered in the disguise of griffins" he adds further.

"Undoubtedly, griffins are place for humans who are ignored and differentiated"

She walks to the dais where they have weekly meetings.

"Ladies and gentlemen, we have new birds in the flock. Let's join and congratulate them in this mission of tearing the skin of serpents"

"Cheers, cheers" were the sounds they were hearing.

Chapter 5

Griffins were loyal and trustworthy only to those who gave importance to their culture and race. Vikram and govind were trying hard to gain their trust and get the information required for investigation. As days passed, they became the legal members of the community and were offered to join the group to wage war on the town. Griffins had community president who is responsible for conducting oath ceremony and providing griffin clothes. On the day of ceremony, they would be offered a glass of wine and a robbed watch as a symbol of unity. These watches were customized after robbing to show their unity and identity from other residents of town.

Soon, president reaches the dais of weekly meetings and addresses the crowd.

"We, the members of town are the real owners of orient hills. Our race was deprived of food, shelter and shown discrimination. We shall get back what we owe until our last breath"

Crowd starts shouting.

"Griffins, Griffins"

"Today we have two new members in the group and let's congratulate them for this divine opportunity" and asks them to repeat the words which were spoken by him.

"We the Griffins would abide by laws of community and get back the lost glory of us, we never back down from any challenge and put our death in front of our goal"

Saying these words, he offered them a glass of wine with griffin clothes and the lady who introduced them to the group is assigned with the task of training them.

As day progresses, pleasant winds move across the town to give residents a beautiful night. Moon starts to appear and shower beautiful moonlight. On the night of oath ceremony, they cook delicious meat and consume wine to enjoy the day. They cooked mountain deer which was hunted illegally from the woods.

Vikram and Govind started to have their supper and beautiful lady introduces herself as emily. Her beautiful eyes and seductive appearance made govind to fall in love with her but vikram was constantly trying to hold him back.

"Hey guys, hope you enjoyed the supper?"

"Yes, we did" govind answered but she didn't get an answer from vikram.

She looks at vikram and asks again.

"And you??"

Here also govind responds saying,

"Yes, he also enjoyed"

She says "can't he respond" then vikram responds saying.

"Yes, I've enjoyed"

"Get back to bed and don't move into the woods without my permission and soon you'll be assigned a task" saying these words she leaves.

Chapter 6

The next day, orient hills witnessed the day which will write the blood words on the silent history of the town. It was so terrifying and haunted; residents couldn't believe it.

The residents of orient hills were shocked by the latest news which prevailed in the town. Town experienced major disturbances in the past, but this is devastating and terrible. The storm was on its way and it's going to disturb every one of the town. Two dead bodies were found on the northern side of hills, an area covered with dense trees, less crowded, and more haunted. Thick trees and waterfall at the centre usually should be a tourist place, but it was haunted with darkness and frequent deaths at similar places shook the entire town.

The river which flows from northern part of town to southern was the silent witness of murders. It flows through the trees and gets dense with additional water which comes from waterfall.

Police officers of the town reached the place with the help of civilians as dead bodies were found in the river.

Two dead bodies pertain to a girl and a boy. Both of them were naked, blood was shattered all over the area. Both of them were killed brutally and it was a horrible gesture to the police officer who was specially appointed to solve the mystery.

Vikram was now in the disguise of griffins and had to reach the place as police officer, so he made a plan to escape from griffin's place and reach the murdered place. He pretends to have a stomach ache and needs a medical emergency, so griffins arrange an emergency cab to the local medical practitioner to cure his ache. He boards the cab and in the pretext of attending nature-call he moves secretly into the woods.

"Could you please stop the cab, nature is calling me" says vikram.

"Sorry sir!"

"I can't, I have a protocol to stop only at the hospital" cab driver confirms.

"Please stop!"

"On human grounds please accept my request" says vikram.

"Okay, but please don't tell anyone about this" says cab driver.

"Sure" and he moves into the woods which were beside roads and from there reach the place of murder.

The sight was so terrible and disgusting as beautiful waters were carrying the blood of dead bodies. Bodies were floating on the river and were naked, immediately he ordered for recovery of bodies and covered them with clothes. He examines the bodies clearly and tries to investigate how the murder took place. Throats and veins of bodies were cut due to which bodies became pale. Additionally, they had signs of skin been torn and this resembled they had severe fight before the murder. There were hand prints around neck and they were stabbed with a knife.

"These bastards are on the game again" says vikram.

"So inhuman and demonic, very soon their inheritance would be stopped" says vikram with a face of anger.

"Yes sir, so inhuman and darker" says one of the subordinates.

Clues team appeared and they try to locate the clues but in vain. The only information they can locate is the hairs from mouths of dead bodies. They collect the hairs and send the bodies to obtain an autopsy report.

Chapter 7

Next day morning, govind tries to find real facts about the incident.

"Did they catch you and made you responsible for the murders" says govind.

"Are you stupid"

"I'm a recognized cop and how can someone make me accept"

"I've made a false story so that they can believe me"

"I went to murdered place to investigate" says vikram.

"Sir, you're amazing!" govind adds.

"Now please be calm and get to work" vikram added again.

Emily made arrangements for the training of vikram and govind and it involves robbing the local train which passes through the orient hills. Orient hills were surrounded by dense forests and the train passes through these forests to reach the surrounding towns. Training involves self-defence, robbery techniques and other mischievous acts which griffins perform. After a month of training, the day has arrived wherein they need to rob the train which contained precious ornaments. These ornaments were made of gold and other precious metals and they would be moved from one town to another connecting orient hills. When the train halts in orient hills for regular activities they need to rob the ornaments.

"I've never imagined a day which could make me involved in robbery" says govind.

"You should be prepared for everything and anything. I guess this was taught in our police academy" vikram adds ironically.

Then both of them burst out laughing.

On the day of the robbery, vikram and govind were drowsy and their level of interest wasn't high. As they were cops, the act of robbery was against their rules but were determined in mission of finding culprits. They were not interested in robbery and seeing this emily wants to ensure they are motivated and complete the tasks assigned.

"I can imagine that you both are nervous as this is the first time you're directly involved in a robbery"

"But nothing comes easy, we've to pour our sweat to get the life which we deserve"

"We're robbing these ornaments not only to protect griffins but to attain financial security for our children"

"let's be focused and achieve the task assigned" says emily.

Hearing these words both pretend to be motivated and confirms.

"Yes, we will achieve" added by them.

When the train halts in orient hills they rob the ornaments without hurting anyone. This made everyone overwhelmed and they wanted to celebrate this achievement but community head stops them and confirms it's just a robbery and can't be celebrated until bigger one is achieved.

Emily was overjoyed and greets both of them for their first achievement.

"Good job!"

"Certainly!"

"It was not an easy task but you made it look easier" she said.

"You're welcome!!" says vikram.

"It wasn't possible without you" added by govind.

"My pleasure!"

"We will collaborate more in the coming future" she adds and then leaves for the night.

Chapter 8

"Broken faith's, disturbed minds and unsolved mysteries, orient hills were beaten badly. Customs and traditions were at stake and dark mysteries prevailed in the town"

"The blood sheds, killings near lonely highway, and dead bodies in the river resonate deadly nature of murderers and residents were vacating the town"

"I'm pissed off, unable to find a single clue which could lead to my destiny" vikram utters.

"Sir, don't worry!"

"We are on the right track" says govind.

"One clue could redefine our investigation" he replies with a pathetic face.

As these conversations continue emily makes herself available and provides them one crucial task to be completed.

"Hey guys!"

"Are you busy, aren't you?"

"We are not" vikram confirms.

"Okay, we have a crucial task to be performed and this order came from the community head" she says.

Both of them started imagining what could be the tasks. They start to release those ideas upon their wish but emily stops them as it was ruining time.

"Hold on!"

"I know how curious you are, but please hold on to your horses" says emily.

"Let me grab the map of orient hills"

She pulls the map out of her pocket and spreads on the table.

"Orient hills are divided into two parts, the northern and the southern one's. The river flows from the northern part to the southern part and we have the woods which are besides the river. Even we have a highway which is deserted and this will take us to the hills in the northern part" she adds.

"A highway which is deserted??" govind says.

"Oh, yeah!"

"The residents call it a lonely highway" emily adds and she continues further.

"We're going to hills in the northern part using the lonely highway which starts from the middle of the town. We are using the highway because it is deserted and police patrolling would start only after night. Before patrolling we reach there and obtain marijuana.

After that we reach the woods which are besides the river and slowly travel through the river using a boat which is already arranged. Then we reach our place which is in the southern part. This is very crucial because marijuana is the primary source of our income" saying these words she concludes.

"Do you know who gave this order to the community head??" vikram questions.

"I'm not sure"

"I'm here only to follow protocols and do my job" she adds.

"But you should also know how our actions impact others" says vikram.

"Agreed!"

"But that's not my concern and let's focus on the job" saying these words she moves on.

Chapter 9

As per the plan they reach the hills which is in the northern part and obtain marijuana which is a dangerous drug. Then they carry the drug with them using the boat which was already arranged. Indeed, the plan went smoothly until they were stopped by the cops who were doing night patrolling. When they were travelling in the river carrying marijuana, they were noticed by few cops who threw light on them to see their faces. As it was dark in the evening, their faces were not visible clearly. They ask them to stop and wants to verify the boat.

"Hey"

"you guys"

"Stop!"

"Stop!"

"It's an order!"

"Otherwise, you'll be shot"

Boat has to be stopped otherwise cops would start firing. Vikram and govind didn't have much time and they move the boat towards the river edge beside the woods. They step down from the boat and their faces slowly appear in the moon light. When cops see their faces, it was a kind of surprise to see them as griffins.

"Sir!"

"Nice to meet you"

"Are you performing an operation?" and they start to salute them.

Emily watches everything from the boat as she didn't step down yet.

"Idiot!"

"Go away from here" vikram says with a frustrated face. They didn't have an idea of the plan and starts saluting govind too.

Emily observes and comes to the conclusion that govind and vikram aren't orphans but the cops who came to destroy their goals. Immediately, she becomes active and moves the boat faster into the river so that she can escape from the place.

Govind and vikram fires bullets in the air but she didn't stop.

"You, idiots"

"You've destroyed our plan"

"Now let's call everyone to catch the griffins" says vikram with loud words.

Soon vikram with his team reach griffins place and orders everyone to surrender. He carries a megaphone speaker and orders them to surrender.

"I can understand your agony and feelings of not being valued"

"If you surrender, I'll ensure you become the residents of orient hills and lead a peaceful life" says vikram.

"You're a traitor" words pop up from the houses which were used by griffins and these were spoken by emily.

"Yes, traitor"

"Traitors!"

"Traitors!" these were the words spoken by other griffins.

"Please forgive me!"

"I was doing my duty nothing more than that. Someone is trying to use you for a bad cause. You need to stop all these so that you can become legal residents of orient hills" says vikram politely.

"We are griffins and we don't need anyone's help"

"We will get what we owe with guns and bullets" and they start firing.

Vikram and govind were left with no choice except to counter attack. There was firing between two groups, few cops and griffins were dead but ultimately some of them were caught and remaining escaped from there with help of the community head. Emily also got arrested with others, most of them being males. They were handcuffed and moved to the police station where they will be interrogated.

Vikram and his team were successful in arresting few griffins and this was applauded by his superiors. Indeed, the job was risky but he made it look easy. Female cops were assigned to get information from emily which could help him in the investigation.

Emily was moved to a special cell wherein all facilities were arranged on the orders of vikram. He wasn't against her but she was in the wrong group. He came to the cell to explain her about his job and the load he's carrying on his shoulders to find the culprits.

"I know you're really upset with me but I'm helpless and town is at risk with multiple murders" says vikram.

"You're a traitor!"

"You don't have courage to face us" she adds.

"I can make you a legal resident of the town if you can provide some details about the murders"

"I'm only smooth in regards to you as we had some good interactions before"

"If you still won't cooperate with me, you'll be handled in a different way" he adds.

"Go to hell" she adds further with anger on her face.

"I'm here to help you but you aren't supporting me"

"Now face the consequences at your risk" and he moves on.

Emily was passed on to a female cop where she will be interrogated without mercy. Days passed and emily was interrogated in all possible ways but she was not ready to provide any piece of information. Lastly, vikram makes a plan and gets dressed as a griffin to extract the information from her.

"I know we've betrayed you and it was our job. Now I've dressed as you to show respect towards your culture and traditions"

"I came with an offer, if you give me some information, I'll assure all your friends will be freed from charges and made rightful citizens of the town" says vikram.

These words make her feel good as long wished dream comes to reality but she doesn't believe him until he signs an agreement with her duly signed by him. She asked to send a copy of the agreement to the head of the community and this was done quickly. Agreement contained information about disclosing substantial information about the murders in return exchange for valid citizenship for griffins.

She reveals partial evidence which could solve some mystery about these murders.

"The river on the northern side of hills and the woods beside the river can give you few clues which can help you solve these mysteries" says emily.

"Thank you!"

"But what kind of evidence" says vikram.

"I'm not sure but I overheard a few griffins talking" she adds.

"Okay but make sure you provide all the information you have"

"Sure" she adds again.

✳ ✳ ✳

Chapter 10

As per the information provided by emily they reached the river on the northern side of hills and the woods beside to obtain some clues. After detailed investigation of the area they couldn't find any clues but vikram was sure because emily has taken a signed agreement in exchange for information.

"We should get the clues at any instance; this could pave path to solve the murders" says vikram.

"Sure Sir" govind utters and orders his subordinates to investigate the place more precisely.

Govind orders his subordinates to jump into the river and see if they can find something informative. Meanwhile, vikram and govind move into the woods if they could find some clues. As they move deeper, they find few huts in the woods. These huts were very short and showed signs of illegal activities. Indeed, they were very dangerous from outside and when they moved inside, the rotten smell of blood made them uneasy. Huts were used to perform certain demonic poojas with sheeps being sacrificed. It also contained the photo of a demonic god with bangles being offered as part of tantric pooja.

He orders govind to collect all the samples carefully as part of the investigation. As they were busy collecting samples one of the subordinate's rushes and informs, they found something mysterious in the river.

Immediately they rush to the place to verify the mysterious thing, subordinates conclude they found a metal box sealed.

"Why are you wasting time??"

"Extract the box and verify the materials inside" govind orders.

"Sure sir" one of the subordinates responds.

They extract the box and remove the seal and found two bodies inside. Only skeleton was existing with no flesh, but they had the signs of griffins. They wore jacket of griffins and this made him to conclude these bodies pertains to griffins. Samples were collected to send forensic lab for further investigation and bodies were sent for autopsy report.

It was tedious job for forensic team because they got lot of samples and this may consume more time but vikram requested them to make faster as case is becoming complex. Forensic team has provided reports for the first two murders, one was for ivy and jake and other was near lonely highway.

Autopsy report of ivy and jake stated they had two handprints on the bodies. Handprints were existing near neck and leg portions of the bodies. It also stated two or more persons involved based on the handprints.

Additionally, the person who handled legs may be a female because of shorter hands. It also stated there was fierce fight between two groups.

Forensic report stated footprints were different in size and they had peculiar design formed when stepped in, these shoes were not sold in orient hills and stated non-residents were involved in the murders also footprints found in cottage were of different size resembling more than one person involved in the murders.

Autopsy report of murder near lonely highway was also retrieved and in a strange manner there wasn't detailed report. This was suspicious for vikram and it also concluded these civilians were moving in the woods at night and were attacked by wild animals. This was strange for him and ordered for the officer who was in charge for the autopsy.

"Sir, the officer who was transferred to other place due to his family obligations" says govind.

"Certainly, this is an act of someone who's trying to hide the facts" says vikram.

It was evening and he thought of meeting emily to share the news of clues found in the river but it was raining and he couldn't make, so he decides to continue the hunt tomorrow. Vikram and govind were tired and in order to keep themselves refreshed they move to the nearby bar thereafter moving to their nests.

✳ ✳ ✳

Chapter 11

Orient hills were once place for heaven, now due to these murders and illegal activities it became the place for darkness. Monthly journal which was circulated in the town showed the residents about the darkness prevailed in the town. Journal was named as "Nests of orient hills" and it was published by editor abhi, who was migrated from other town to orient hills. One piece of information in journal goes as follows.

"Orient hills, Orient hills"

"Since how many days we didn't had proper sleep?"

"Can't we get peace and prosperity?"

"Every single day we see a murder in the town, it's better we look for another town"

"If we don't get what we demand for, why should we pay taxes"

"Rise, awake, assemble and revolt against police department"

These were the words written in the journal and it also reached vikram which made him anger and he rushed towards editor like an ambush.

"What the hell are you doing??" vikram with anger on face.

"We are trying to restore peace and harmony in the town and you're trying to disturb the same" he adds again.

"Sir, I'm not understanding"

"Could you please reiterate again" abhi with a sense of doubt and confusion.

"The journal which is published by you is against the police department and we aren't keeping the investigation idle"

"Yes, the town is disturbed and at the same time it's not easy to find culprits without proper investigation" he adds further with more anger.

"I'm sorry!"

"I didn't mean to corner the department but wanted to show the real view of the town" abhi adds again.

"Understood!"

"But be careful going forward"

"Sure, and I'll support you in the course of research"

Then vikram makes his way to the jail where emily was kept and he disclosed the clues which he gathered in the river and in the woods.

"We've searched the place suggested by you and found some clues which will be disturbing for you"

She was frightened after hearing these words.

"Could you please conclude clearly as to what you want to convey" she adds.

"We've found two dead bodies sealed in the box and stored in the river; these bodies pertain to griffins" he concludes.

"Dead bodies!"

"Those pertains to griffins" with a face of surprise.

"Yes"

"But what's the need of someone to kill them and store them in a sealed box"

"We are also confused"

"If you would remember something related which could help us in the process"

"Yes, I do remember and two persons were missing from an operation for which I was the head"

"Community head told us that they were in a separate mission" she adds further.

"A separate mission" he adds with a sense of doubt.

"What was that??" he questioned again.

"I didn't know" emily with a tone of dullness.

"No worries"

"Please recollect more if anything is missing"

"Sure"

Then he attends the meeting of higher officials wherein they want to know the progress of the case. Police officials were questioned by higher authorities about the case progress. Vikram made them clear it's a true act of a gang which is trying to make the town an unpeaceful place. He disclosed autopsy reports and other clues which he gathered from different places of the town and he ensured culprits will be caught soon.

Autopsy reports of dead bodies which were naked and forensic report of knife, doll found in the woods near lonely highway was received. It clearly states the handprints on the bodies, doll and the knife are the same and also shorter. The hair which was in the mouth of victims resembles a lady aged between 30 to 35 years.

Day by day the case was getting complicated and it was clear actions by a group of persons. He ordered govind to extract the data of citizens who were aged between 30 to 35 including men so that data is accurate. He also stated he needs the data of shoes which were found in the cottage of ivy and jake so that he can locate manufacturer.

"I need the data very fast without any delay"

"Sure sir" and he sets his journey.

More than four murders, tantric poojas, bloodshed and warnings to him. He was very disturbed and couldn't find himself at the right position but he self-motivated himself to solve the mystery as he was specially appointed to solve the case. He made all pointers on his investigation board so that no information is missed. He orders the map of the town and establishes a connection between the murders, after a heavy brainstorming he could find a pattern for murders. The murder in the woods occurred on 2nd, next murder which is of ivy and jake happened on

4th and the murder of two residents happened on 6th of the respective months, so the next murder would happen on 8th of this month. He grabs the calendar nearby and checks the date and it was shocking for him as 8th is today.

He immediately calls govind and informs him about his analysis and he was convinced too. He assembles his subordinates and sends some to lonely highway and assists few of them to the woods besides river.

Chapter 12

It was a scary night with bright moon in the sky and the town was sleeping with no one outside. Vikram was marching with his troops in order to trace out the murderers. Everyone was sleeping but police personnel were at the place of risk in order to save town. Govind with his men were patrolling near lonely highway and vikram was assisted by few cops besides the river.

Suddenly he could hear sounds of screaming in the woods.

"Help"

"Help"

He rushed with his team and sounds came deeper from the woods and they switched on the torches brought by them. Lights were penetrating from the torches and this was seen by the persons who were screaming. They had stabs of knife but escaped by the grace of god.

"Arrest those bastards and bring to me" vikram orders his men. His men marched inside the forest firing and found two men masked with dangerous knife and axe in their hands. They fired in the air stating to surrender.

"Surrender yourself either you'll be killed without mercy" they've surrounded the murderers and passed orders with guns aiming towards their hearts.

Murderers were silent for 20 seconds with no action showing their harmless behaviour but in one instance they started attacking cops with their knives and axe. Cops had no choice and fired at them in which one was killed and other wounded severely. Wounded person was taken to hospital nearby as he will pave the path to find culprits.

"You're in safe hands" says vikram to the persons who escaped from murderers.

These persons were travelling along the lonely highway but were saved by the intelligence of vikram.

Govind was busy in gathering the data of persons who were aged 30 to 35 and also the manufacturer of shoes. It wasn't easy for him as the data was complex and large. He approached the municipality of orient hills and requested for the persons who are aged between 30 to 35. Local body of government provides the data and it consists of 100 persons out of which 40 persons were females. In order to retrieve the data about the manufacturer, he approached local residents who were working for the police department. Meanwhile, govind provides the data to vikram for his review.

"Sir, we got the data of persons who are aged between 30 to 35" says govind.

"Perfect!"

"Data is accurate, isn't it??" vikram posed a question.

"Yes, it's accurate because I've gathered from the local municipality"

"Total 100 persons aged between 30 to 35 out of that 40 are females"

"Awesome!"

"Send our men to their houses and ask them to come for an informal talk"

"Sure Sir"

As instructed his men went to 40 houses with addresses provided by govind. They explained the issues which are faced by town and informed them they should come for an informal talk, similarly they were going for all the houses but when they reach last house which is 40th one, they observe house was locked. Cops interrogated the house which was beside and got to know it was vacant for entire month. They broke in and searched house thereby finding a pair of shoes which had similar design found in cottage of ivy and jake. Details were passed to govind so that they can review.

Govind calls vikram and cascades with a sign of an achievement.

"We've got a vital breakthrough in the case" govind with a strong voice.

"Awesome"

"What's the clue??"

"Our men searched for the female residents with the data and one of the houses was sealed but when broke in found a pair of shoes which had same design found in the cottage"

"Fantastic!"

vikram applauds their work.

"How about the manufacturer??" he questioned again.

"They are on the hunt and we will get the details soon" govind confirms.

"Okay, let me know once you receive information" says vikram and he was in his house.

It was the month of November; winter season was very high making everyone in the town to shiver but the wine which was produced in the town is a perfect remedy to keep town shelters warm. Maple wine was produced in the town and was a profitable business for certain businessmen in the town. Maple trees were found in large numbers to the northern side of the hills. Nobody cultivated these trees but they were formed naturally in the hills by nature and some robbers illegally used the trees for making wine hence the government of orient hills decided to sell the trees in small quantities to selected businessmen.

It was cold morning and winds across the town made town even colder. Even snowfall was very high in the town and it made town look an iceberg in the antarctica, roads were blocked with ice which caused inconvenience for daily activities. Municipality workers were trying hard to clear the snow so that they are no accidents. He was in the room with his jacket worn and consumed a glass of maple wine to keep himself warm. He prepared a bread omelette and ate within an hour then he wore the dress of his duty so that he can march on his mission.

His car suffered the cold whole night and engine couldn't start but after long try it starts and his mobile rings with his mom's number.

"How did you answer the call at first instance?"

"It's a sense of achievement for me" his mom says ironically.

"Mom, I'm pissed off with this case and it's draining me completely"

"Please understand and I'll return once case is solved" says vikram with frustration on his face.

"That's the reason I've asked you to quit the job"

"Mom, please stop!"

"Please take care of your health and have the pills on time"

"I'll send the money to your account and I also reached out to our housekeeper, he'll take care you and home"

"Hmmm"

"Please take care of your health" his mom says finally with no words left.

"Sure mom!" and he disconnects the call.

Chapter 13

He enters the car and starts towards police station, govind was already existing in the place. Doctors provided proper treatment to the person who was wounded in the woods and now he can speak to others.

"The wounded persons opened his eyes and we can get some information from him"

"Sure, let's go and find something related to the case" says vikram.

Both of them reach the hospital and he was very fatigue. They have received confirmation from doctor to interrogate the person.

"I know you're wounded badly"

"I'm here to help you"

"I can you reduce your time in jail if you support us"

He was unable to respond properly and with a mild voice he says "Sure" and continues.

"We were poor, downtrodden and our family lead miserable lives. We want to live luxurious life but became prey for the desires. On a sunny day my family visited local gathering which was conducted in the community hall. We went to take free eye test which was conducted by government officials and found a person named "Maddy". I've became victim for his activities, at first, he assigned us tiny activities to make the people frightened who pass by the lonely highway making strange sounds and he offered good amount of money. Later on, greediness increased within us and wanted to make more money which made us do ill-legal activities. He offered to kill the couples who were passing highway and thus terrorizing the town. On his note we killed a couple and dragged them into the woods hanging them to trees and offered fake tantric poojas. We were doing similar act on the day but you caught us"

"What's the motive of these activities??" vikram questions.

"I've asked them on multiple occasions but they warned us to stay away from these types of investigations"

He was in his early teens and the greediness of money made him a murderer.

"What's your age??" govind questions again.

"16 years" he responds.

After inquiring more and recording his statements he was moved to juvenile custody.

Govind was busy in finding the data about manufacturer, the footprints of the shoes found in the cottage. The cops who were sent to search the manufacturer had returned with the data and it was vital for the progress of the case. These shoes were manufactured by a shoe company in the town besides orient hills. It was adjacent to orient hills and was the source of all illegal activities. Maple wine produced in orient hills had huge demand in the adjacent town which was called "Vale hills". Vikram was delighted as his investigation was on the right track and soon culprits would be caught and sent behind bars. Vikram obtains permission from his superiors to investigate the company in vale hills.

"Sir, we've got a lead in the vale hills" vikram to his superior.

"Fabulous!"

"So, what type of support do you need??"

"I need a written document stating permission is granted to investigate the company which produced the shoes" says vikram.

"Sure"

"You'll get your documents in the noon"

"Hope you're fine with the time"

"Sure Sir!"

"Thank you for the confirmation" and he leaves the chamber.

He obtains the documents and travels to vale hills with govind. Vale hills was similar to orient hills but didn't possess mountains and other landscapes. It was covered with large forest and tiny amount of land to reside. When he reached vale hills weather was dry and it wasn't pleasant welcome for him in the station. Police station was untidy and it had large bunch of files which were pending to be actioned. Files were piled up and resembled how crime rate was increased. He submitted the document to authorities so that he can investigate the company.

Chapter 14

The company was well reputed in the town and most of the customers are from both towns. Vikram and govind reached management of the company and tried to extract the information from them. They got a chance to interact with the sales manager of the company.

"Hi Sir!" sales manager greets vikram with a smile on his face.

"Hi"

"Nice to meet you"

"What's your good name??" vikram questions.

"Sir, my name is anmol"

"Pleasure meeting you" he responds.

"How can I help you" he adds again with a polite tone.

"We are from police department of orient hills and he is govind who is subordinate to me"

"Hi Sir!" anmol to govind.

"Hi anmol" govind utters, then vikram jumps into conversation.

"There's a murder which occurred in orient hills and we've certain footprints of murderers which had a unique design of shoes which they wore"

"In our preliminary analysis we noticed these shoes are produced by you"

Govind grabs the photographs of footprints and provides to anmol for his review. When he observed them, it resembles the one's manufactured last year.

"Yes, we've produced this last year but stopped production due to less sales" says anmol.

"Can we know who took orders from you"

"I meant the retailers"

"Definitely, but these aren't sold in orient hills"

"They are sold only in vale hills"

They were shocked because murder of ivy and jake happened in orient hills and no one purchased the product in orient hills. They assumed someone might have travelled from orient hills to vale hills to purchase the product. Govind asked to extract the sales register so that they can find the retailers. As noted, anmol opened sales register and observes shoes were purchased by 10 retailers. As the count of retailers was high, they decided to proceed with each retailer on a daily basis. They were on the hunt to find the murderers and stop these killings in the town. The process of finding them was very tough as they were intelligent and expert in these activities. They searched the shops but it was in vain and couldn't find any data related to murders. Sales data was demanded but it contained only a few customers and they were not repeatedly purchasing the shoes. It was the last shop and tenth one wherein they were searching for their last hope. Sales book was maintained by the retailer in an accurate manner making their job easy. When they searched the data for the last 3 years, found one person who was purchasing the product constantly. He was the only consumer of the product in the last 3 years and it caused some sense of doubt for them. They took the mobile number and address from the sheet and went to his house.

Next day, they reach the place of the person with the address in the sales register. The place was far away from town and only few houses found in the street. Street was untidy and had no proper maintenance by the government. Passing through the streets they reach the house they intended but it was locked. Vikram investigates the house completely from the front and back to locate something useful. It had a garden in the front and water well in the backside. House was perfect example for haunted house. Govind tries to gather some information from the neighbours. Vikram peeps inside the well and sees a disturbing sight which wasn't a good sign for the case. There was a dead body floating inside the well and he was shocked, he extracts the body with the help of nearby neighbours. It was a male person and contained mighty injury on his head. It resembled someone hit him on the head with great force. They also found a rock nearby which had blood on it and thus it was concluded person was killed using the rock. Govind asks neighbours about his personal details. They state him as "Maddy" and this makes both of them sad as they lost a precious breakthrough in the case. It was a perfect lead to find the person behind these murders. They also received information about his wife angel who was a drug addict. Maddy and angel both had sleepless nights due to the quarrels they had for multiple reasons. Maddy was a thief but was kind hearted in donating the money to the needy. Maddy tried to change angel about her habits but she was stubborn and had regular fights with him. They broke the entrance door and went inside the house to see if they could find something vital. Rooms were very untidy with a rotten smell and no proper ventilation. They see the photographs of the couple and take them into their bags which they carried. They were not responsible for an autopsy report because it was vale hills, they made a call to the cops and they landed without wasting any time. Meanwhile, they also tried to get information on angel as she's not there in the place. Nobody provided information about her as she wasn't socially involved with others but her absence was strange and suspicious. Additionally, they found the shoes which had similar footprints of shoes found in the cottage. Now they are clear, couple had some connection with these murders.

"Sir, it resembles someone is following us" says govind.

"Yes, even I think so" vikram responds.

"Let's keep an eye on the surroundings and people" he adds again.

"We will conduct autopsy reports to the body and provide you the report" says the local cop.

"Sure!"

"That helps us"

"If you need any sort of help, please feel free to ask"

"Sure"

"Thank you" vikram concludes.

When everything went as per protocols they drive back to hotel where they were staying. Day by day intent to find the culprits was increasing and now investigation was on the right track.

Chapter 15

Angel was suspicious person in the murder of maddy as she has gone missing on the day of murder. Police officials of vale hills were assigned to arrest her along with the cops of orient hills. Photographs of couple were circulated in local newspapers of orient and vale hills. Nests of orient hills published the information about maddy and angel claiming if anyone finds angel, they can contact vikram. Mobile number of vikram was also listed in the article to contact in case anyone find suspects. Meanwhile, vikram orders for the CCTV footage across the streets they travelled till they reach home of maddy. Govind made himself busy in extracting the footage going to nearby shops and retailers whom they investigated. Govind finds someone suspicious who was hiding behind a bus while vikram and govind investigating last retailer. When they analyse the video, it was shocking for them as it was maddy who was following.

Govind rushed towards vikram with the footage and his notes.

"Sir, we've found the person who was following us"

"Great!"

"Who is that??" vikram questioned.

"It was maddy himself" he responded.

"Are you crazy??"

"It's impossible"

"That's true" he claims again showing the footage.

"Murderer is playing extremely well and moving ahead of us". We need to act smart before he outsmarts us" vikram says with his brave heart.

Higher official of vikram was serious with his act of revealing photographs of suspects but he was left with no choice. He wanted murders to cease immediately so that both towns should be a safe place for living.

He was questioned about his act of revealing the photographs.

"We know you're best in the business but revealing the photos of suspects isn't an ideal option" superior to vikram.

"Indeed, I've broken the protocol but left with no choice"

"We need to cease the murders otherwise orient hills would become a desert with no residents" vikram adds.

"We can understand but justify your actions arresting the culprits"

"Sure Sir!"

"Definitely we will show the power of cops"

Superior wasn't happy with his actions but they had no choice except for him because he holds good amount of information regarding the case. As call ended, he receives another one stating they've found angel in orient hills. The caller was from orient hills and he had a clear information about angel.

"Hello" says the person.

"Hello" vikram utters.

"Can I speak to vikram"

"You're speaking with vikram, please proceed"

"Sir, I've seen the lady listed in the newspaper "nests of orient hills"

"She's residing in a home far away from town and I'll send the address to your mobile"

"That's great!"

"Please watch her activities and keep us informing every hour"

"We are on the way and will reach tonight"

"Definitely!" person responds.

Vikram alerts his team and moves towards the orient hills. Distance between both towns was long and it took more time to reach the place. It was night till they reached the town and he ordered his team to surround the house with no one disturbed. The place was far away from the town and showed lack of development.

Govind was shocked seeing the house as it was the same house which his subordinates broke in to find the female suspects. It was the same 40th house of female aged 30 to 35 in which they found the shoes which led to vale hills.

They were some sounds inside the house which made vikram and his team to be attentive. They could hear someone singing a song with a scary dance. When they moved further, she was consuming "marijuana" and was high on it in the state of illusion. Vikram ordered his female subordinates to arrest her and as per the orders they charge inside. Even though she was high in "marijuana", angel tried to attack cops with knife which she always carried. Female cops were expert in handling these cases, they hit her hard with guns carried and she became unconscious. She was handcuffed and moved into custody for further investigation.

Chapter 16

She's the prime suspect in murder of ivy and jake as footprints formed by shoes resembles with the same shoes found in house of angel. Vikram conveys messages to superior officials and requests for higher protection as suspect would be harmed. As per the request protection force was increased. Vikram prepared a set of questionnaires to investigate angel but unfortunately, they received another obstacle from griffins. A warning letter was attached on the notice board of police station and it was done before cops arrived to perform their duties. It contained deadly warning from community head and it goes as follows.

"We're the true saviours of the town and legal owners of the town. Angel is a griffin and you can't arrest her without our intent. She's innocent and in this cause, you're trying to save the businessmen who are the real culprits"

"Release her and emily without any constraints otherwise we'll show your fate"

Vikram was serious on the note and doesn't understand why griffins are trying to save the culprits.

Griffins were serious about the act of arresting their members. They are preparing a plan to set them free.

Two groups had a brutal fight on the day of arresting Emily, griffins moved far away into the woods of maple trees. Maple trees formed as their source of income, they started preparing maple wine and sending them to vale hills. Maple wine had a good consumer base in vale hills hence all businessmen of orient hills want to acquire northern hills. Presently, griffins were taking shelters in maple woods making temporary huts. Community head was heading them and inspired them with a powerful speech.

"We own this land, every rock, tree, and every inch of land belongs to us. Let's wage a war on our enemies and take back our assets. We shall start the journey by making emily and angel free" community head with a loud voice aiming every member of the group.

"Let's make our race the supreme authority of orient hills" says one of the members who got inspired by the words of the community head.

"Griffins!"

"Griffins!" and the crowd starts shouting with these words.

Community head made a plan to attack the jail and police station simultaneously so that they don't have enough time to communicate. They carried barrels of petrol, and guns to fire. They made cotton rolls attached to a wooden stick which will be soaked in petrol and lit the fire to it, then those sticks would be thrown into the station and jail. They also carried leaves of few medicinal plants which are highly toxic, these leaves when burnt produce a smoke which would make unconscious for few minutes. Heavy trucks were used which were robbed by them and they loaded with all the materials gathered. Vikram was in the assumption it was a just a warning to make them scared but didn't predict a heavy hurricane is on the way to destroy them.

Next day around 7 AM, community head with his troops march towards the police to acquire what they believed in, they made a plan to attack them by 9 AM. As per the plan they attack the jail and police station leaving them no options but department was good enough to give them tough fight.

Fierce battle between two groups makes the battleground with blood shed, both groups had severe injuries and few of them got killed. As it was well planned attack emily was removed from the jail and now she's a free bird. Vikram and his team at the police station were efficient enough to stop griffins but more than 5 cops lost their life with few of them wounded in which vikram was the one. Griffins tried their best to save the angel but it wasn't their day. They left the place with emily and the community head was very upset as they couldn't save angel.

Chapter 17

"Nests of orient hills" published an article about the incident which took place in the town. Article supported police department as they sacrificed their lives in safeguarding the town. "Our town had secret enemies, disturbed minds and criminals but police personnel had sacrificed their lives in safeguarding us. We can't bring back the persons who left us but we will support you until real culprits are found. You're the real heroes of the town". Every corner of the town read the article and was impressed with the job of cops. Community head also read the article but was not happy with his team.

"They aren't heroes of the town; we are the ones and will make them villains soon"

Higher officials weren't happy with vikram as he couldn't predict the warning of griffins. He could have suspended but they were left with no choice as vikram had every piece of information regarding the case. They ordered him to close the case as soon as possible. Everyone was aware of the attack due to the article in journal and it got published in other newspapers. Mom of vikram was very tensed hearing the news and she immediately reached orient hills to check the safety of her son.

Vikram and his team were taking treatment in the local hospital for the injuries and she reached their crying all the way. She bursts out crying more when she sees vikram.

"How are you, my son??"

"I know the outcome of this job; hence I asked you to leave much earlier than these possibilities"

"You're the only one I have in my life"

"Quit the job immediately" she says these words with tears rolling out of her eyes.

"Mom, I can understand your pain"

"It's my job and I don't know any other work"

"These are minimal injuries and now I'm fine with the treatment provided"

"Now please leave the place as it's not safe for you" vikram with mild words.

"I can't let you do this job anymore"

"Please quit the job and we will leave this town" she utters again.

"I'm really sorry, I can't leave as I'm responsible for solving the case"

"Okay, will you leave the job after this case" she adds again.

"Yes, I'll do" he lies to her and he asked govind to drop her safely in home. Then she left the place without happiness taking confirmation he would take care of himself.

Attack on cops was major incident in the case as it reveals strange connection to the town and the case. Now angel is the only clue which could solve all the mysteries. He made all arrangements for interrogating angel. She was a drug addict and couldn't sustain without consuming daily. Her health was deteriorating as she didn't consume marijuana. Vikram prepared the questionnaire for the interrogation.

He informed govind to safeguard police station and other cops during course of investigation. She was moved into the interrogation cell but was assisted with few female cops and he started the interrogation. He started investigation politely so that there is no violence.

"I know you're not keeping good, if you support us, we will provide proper food and shelter"

"Also, we will give you proper life making you free from all charges levied" says vikram.

"I don't have any clue of what you're talking"

"I'm innocent and please leave me"

"My husband is dead and you're trying to make me murderer for that, you're nuts" and started crying.

"We didn't try to plot you in the murder of your husband"

"Maddy is killed and you're not in the home" "Could you justify??" he says logically.

"We have two houses; one is in the orient hills and other in vale hills. I came here one day before he was murdered, reason for my travel is to meet a friend"

"Then why did you attack us having marijuana" he questioned again.

"Yes, I'm a drug addict and thought someone tried to attack me hence I've counter attacked"

"I know it's a fable story, if you won't provide accurate data you'll be at stake"

"I'll be back in two hours and make sure you're ready otherwise you'll face the consequences" vikram with anger on his face.

Chapter 18

He calls for the autopsy reports of maddy on an urgent basis. Vikram ordered them to extract handprints of the angel along with personal details for further investigation. Autopsy of maddy was conducted and reports were sent to vikram. Govind extracted handprints of angel along with the personal details. Govind and vikram examined the reports generated and it was shocking for them. Dead body of maddy contained handprints of angel and thus they concluded she was the one who killed him. Additionally personal details of angel were collected from her school which showed her strange behaviour in schooling, she was arrogant and had bad attitude towards others. Her attitude towards society was bad as she lost her mother in an accident wherein no one came to rescue her mother. Sudden demise of her mother had a psychological impact on her and got influenced with ideology of griffins. Later on, she got addicted to drugs and involved herself in crimes but vikram wasn't convinced on how a woman can kill her own husband.

He was more suspicious on angel and her activities in the town. He remembers the autopsy reports of dead bodies which were naked along with knife and doll which were found in the woods near lonely highway. It stated handprints were short and murderer was aged 30 to 35.

He asked govind to extract the files of autopsies which contained handprints and match with of the angel.

"Please match the handprints of angel with other autopsies like naked dead bodies and a doll with knife" he orders.

"Definitely Sir!" and he moved on.

After two hours he again starts interrogation with female cops.

"Now you're in a big risk"

"We know you've murdered maddy but we aren't sure of the intention behind this" he says looking at her face.

"If you cooperate and reveal the truths, we can help you" he adds again.

"I have no idea"

"Go to hell" with anger on her face.

With no choice he asked female cops to start different levels of interrogation, she was treated with second and third degrees but no answer came out of her mouth.

Lastly with no choice he becomes brutal and says "I know the childhood of you, you've been betrayed by the society. I can reduce your crime and make legal resident of orient hills. I'll ensure a law is also passed so that griffins hold a good life once they're included in orient hills. On other hand we have the details like your handprints which match with those found on dead body of maddy"

These words make her emotional and she starts revealing the information. He asked one of the cops to record the statement.

"It all started from my childhood, I was ignored by the society and no one came for the rescue of my mom when she met with an accident. I got influenced with ideology of griffins and later on got addicted to drugs. When I started doing robbery from the train which travelled from vale hills to orient hills, I met maddy who was a regular passenger in the train. He was charming and kind hearted due to which I fell for him. One fine day I proposed him and he accepted on the condition that I should leave drugs. We got married but I couldn't control my habit of consuming drugs and we quarrelled for the same reason"

"Days passed and our domestic life was becoming worse and maddy stopped me from consuming drugs. My health was deteriorating day by day without drugs, he didn't have any choice except to provide drugs to me. When he approached head of community to provide drugs, our situation was misused and he made a deal to provide drugs only when their orders are obeyed. He became helpless and accepted for everything. Firstly, he ordered us to kill ivy and jake because they were foreigners and had no relatives to verify their death"

Everyone was shocked including vikram as he couldn't believe head of the community ordered to kill ivy and jake. He quenched his thirst by a glass of water.

"Why did he wanted to kill those innocent foreigners??" vikram questioned.

"I'm not sure, but also asked to kill a boy and girl who were frequently moving in the woods" angel says again.

"How can we trust your words??" he says with a sense of doubt.

Govind appeared and claimed whatever angel confessed was true.

Chapter 19

"Sir, handprints of angel match with the autopsies reports generated" govind adds.

Then vikram believed firmly she killed those innocent people of the town.

"I have few more doubts, why did you have two houses in different towns??"

"I'm a resident of orient hills and maddy was from vale hills"

"We spent few days in both the towns but the shoes worn by us left the clue unknowingly" she adds crying.

"Maddy hired few people to kill the couple near lonely highway"

"Yes, it was for me in order to obtain drugs"

"Head of the community ordered him to kill them in exchange for drugs"

"Okay" says vikram with a disgusting voice.

"Then what made you kill maddy?"

"We had information of your investigation and he followed you all the way"

"He was scared of being caught and tried to convince me so that we can confess"

"I begged him no to do but he didn't listen"

"Then I hit him with the rock nearby to make him unconscious but he died accidentally. In order to save myself I threw him in the well" and she falls down from the chair sobbing.

Female cops hold her and brings back to normal stage by offering her a glass of water. Govind applauds vikram and claims the case is solved but he stopped him by saying.

"True murderer is yet to be caught and he is the community head"

"He's the real gamer in the play"

"He's using innocent people like griffins for some bad cause" he adds poignantly.

"In the cottage, a ladder also used and their eyes were peeled off"

"You were so demonic!" he says with anger on face.

"We murdered them but eyes were peeled off by others"

"It was raining heavily and hence those footprints were formed due to mud but those people didn't wear any shoes"

"Who are those people??" he questioned again.

"Personal assistants of head of community, they're responsible for creating chaos in the town. They hanged bodies of goats near a lonely highway and warned you on multiple occasions to stay away. They also did tantric poojas and other evil activities in the town" angel says crying.

"Griffins are inhumane and useless. I thought they were fighting for their rights"

"They're innocent but community head is the one who is misusing them for some dirty reasons" she adds.

The real murderer and the person behind these crimes was community head. He was sure angel would disclose the truths and was scared, hence he made attacks on jail and police station so that he can make them free. If they open the mouth dark secrets of his activities would be known to everyone. Vikram conveys information to higher officials and concludes murderer to be community head of griffins. He obtains an arrest warrant and charges like a bull towards the northern hills of orient hills.

He carried his best men in the department to arrest the community head. As a prominent person of griffins, it'll not be an easy task for them but he made a wise plan in order to arrest him. He reached maple woods and sent a statement with one of his subordinates that angel killed herself in order to save the real murderer. He asked angel for the help to pretend as if she was dead and he convinced her in exchange of additional benefits in the town after her release. Vikram told them they came to handover the body as they're the right persons to conduct her funeral. As per the plan community head fell for his trap and came to maple woods with his troops. When he saw the dead body of angel, he pretends crying.

"You're real griffin!"

"You've sacrificed for a good cause" he falls down sobbing.

Immediately, vikram alerts his team and he removes his gun pointing towards his head.

He shouts "Everyone calm down, otherwise I'll shoot him" saying these words he handcuffed him and takes towards the jeep and moves him inside, then he tied him inside the jeep to the rod which was hard to break. His subordinates cover griffins with guns towards them.

"I know you're innocent, your captain is the real culprit for all the murders. We will present him in the court of law for further proceedings, now you can disperse and if you try to counter attack we will ensure you'll be killed without any mercy. You can disperse and I'll ensure every griffin will get legal residency in the town and become good citizens"

When they hear these words their dream of becoming a resident was in front of their eyes and they left the place without any violence. Angel opened her eyes and she was also handcuffed and moved into the jeep.

Angel's addiction towards drugs made maddy and her murderers. Also, she lost the life of maddy to compensate for the evil inside her.

Head of the community was presented before the magistrate and permission was obtained to investigate him. Vikram collects all the evidence against him so that there are no chances to escape.

Head of the community was moved to a separate cell wherein he will be grilled for obtaining information. Special arrangements were made by the police department so that there was no disturbance in the town. Few cops of police department weren't serious about the case and spread the news in the town but vikram and his team ensured murderer is safe so that real truths are revealed.

Vikram ordered govind to ensure culprit is safe and he would start investigation next day with all documents on file. Next day vikram was in police station with evidences collected against him.

"So, you're the murderer and the reason for all crimes in the town" vikram says with his gun pointing towards head of community.

"You've mistaken and going on the wrong path" says head of the community.

"Shut up!" "Shut up!"

"You're are a monster"

"Tried to kill innocent people for your interests"

"If you disclose the truth, you'll be a safe otherwise we'll show the right path" says vikram.

"I'm innocent and I'll talk to my advocate" he utters again.

Vikram was totally pissed off and brings punches on his face with great force. Punch was so strong that he couldn't bear and falls down. Subordinates of vikram holds him and brings back to normal stage.

"If you won't reveal the truth, I'll ensure you'll receive treatment for the bad things made and those would be much worse"

Then he takes a break of 20 mins and gives him those minutes to take final decision.

Chapter 20

He returned after his break and questioned him again. "Are you ready??"

But there was no answer from him and with frustration he drags him to the wall with gun pointing at him.

"I have all the evidence against you"

"It's just I'm doing final confirmation, if you won't reveal the truth, I'll kill you and make myself free from been self-defence" vikram with angered face.

After the warning he gets scared and starts revealing the truth.

"I belonged to a smaller comunity of orient hills where my dad was a daily worker. Mom was a housewife and she died in my childhood suffering my deficiency disease. We didn't have proper protein food due to which I lost my mother. My father got addicted to alcohol and died eventually, that day I've decided to earn money and become rich but it was hard for me to obtain job. This made me to take other direction wherein I've started smuggling drugs and robbing the passengers in train but my thirst for money didn't reduce. One day I heard the value of maple trees found in hills of northern region. Those trees are treasure house of orient hills as maple wine made of it had huge demand in vale hills but those trees are governed by the local body and were in the hands of few businessmen. Hence, I made a plan to become rich by being the sole owner of those trees. In order to obtain those trees, I should have some force and hence I joined griffins as one of the members. Day by day I've gained their trust and eventually became head of the community. I used hatred in the hearts of griffins against orient hills to achieve my dream. My plan is to conduct evil activities in town like tantric poojas, dolls with knife, other demonic things so that residents of town are scared and they leave the town. Then I would become supreme authority of the town and conduct my business. It went for a few months but it didn't work hence I started killing residents with the help of maddy and angel using their weakness. I maintained some personal assistants who were responsible for conducting these evil and demonic activities in the town"

"Does griffins know about your activities??" vikram questioned.

"No, they're innocent and didn't have any clue about these activities. After town becomes empty, I wanted to make griffins legal residents of orient hills and use them for my purpose"

"Head of the community was a mask for my evil activities and griffins were resources to obtain them. I wanted to increase hatred in hearts of griffins and use that hatred for my own gains"

"I told them we need to make orient hills empty by scaring the town and used them for conducting robbery, smuggling and tantric poojas but on the other hand my real intention is to make profits by selling precious maple wine"

"You're such a bad guy with no good deeds"

"Then who murdered griffins and sealed them in a metal box stored in the river??" vikram questioned again.

"I've murdered them because when I was performing tantric poojas in the huts they crossed my area and messed with me"

"Being supreme authority of griffins, I've tried to explain them but they were reluctant to listen to my words"

"This made me to kill them and if their bodies are found by the community, they would research and find me hence I stored in the metal box" community head cries out loudly.

"I've tried to free angel from police station so that my secrets aren't disclosed but you gathered information from angel" he says with a dull voice.

"You're so inhuman and will pay for your actions" says vikram.

Vikram with all the evidences presents him in the court of law. After lawful proceedings in the court, law authority decided to provide life time imprisonment to the community head and was sent behind bars. Then after a few days orient hills was on the right track with no disturbance. Residents who left the town returned and were leading peaceful lives. Vikram and govind were given promotion and charges which were against griffins was lifted. As promised vikram ensured griffins were provided legal residency of orient hills.

Angel was provided good treatment to forget her addiction and was also made legal resident of the town.